CUSTOMER SERVICE EXCELLENCE

Libraries & Archives

Kent
County
Council

# My Secret Unicorn

## Friends Forever

# Linda Chapman

*Illustrated by Ann Kronheimer*

**PUFFIN**

PUFFIN BOOKS

Published by the Penguin Group
Penguin Books Ltd, 80 Strand, London WC2R ORL, England
Penguin Group (USA) Inc., 375 Hudson Street, New York, New York 10014, USA
Penguin Group (Canada), 90 Eglinton Avenue East, Suite 700, Toronto, Ontario,
Canada M4P 2Y3 (a division of Pearson Penguin Canada Inc.)
Penguin Ireland, 25 St Stephen's Green, Dublin 2, Ireland
(a division of Penguin Books Ltd)
Penguin Group (Australia), 250 Camberwell Road, Camberwell, Victoria 3124, Australia
(a division of Pearson Australia Group Pty Ltd)
Penguin Books India Pvt Ltd, 11 Community Centre, Panchsheel Park,
New Delhi – 110 017, India
Penguin Group (NZ), cnr Airborne and Rosedale Roads, Albany, Auckland 1310,
New Zealand (a division of Pearson New Zealand Ltd)
Penguin Books (South Africa) (Pty) Ltd, 24 Sturdee Avenue, Rosebank,
Johannesburg 2196, South Africa

Penguin Books Ltd, Registered Offices: 80 Strand, London WC2R ORL, England

www.penguin.com

First published 2006
1

Text copyright © Working Partners Ltd, 2006
Illustrations copyright © Ann Kronheimer, 2006
All rights reserved

The moral right of the author and illustrator has been asserted

Typeset in Bembo by Palimpsest Book Production Limited, Polmont, Stirlingshire

Made and printed in England by Clays Ltd, St Ives plc

British Library Cataloguing in Publication Data
A CIP catalogue record for this book is available from the British Library

ISBN-13: 978–0–141–32024–3
ISBN-10: 0–141–32024–9

*To the real Jasmine, Rose and Natasha*

# CHAPTER
# One

'Are you ready, Twilight?' Lauren
whispered.

Twilight nodded. 'Yes.' He touched his
glittering silver horn to the rock of rose
quartz on the ground before them. 'Cedar
Creek Riding Camp!' he declared.

A purple mist swirled over the rock
and its pinky-grey surface began to shine
like a mirror. As the smoke cleared,

Lauren saw a picture appearing. It showed a large grassy campsite with a horse barn, paddocks, three white cabins with window boxes full of flowers and a long low central building. Dark woods fringed the fields. Through them, Lauren could see the silvery gleam of a creek in the moonlight.

'Oh, wow!' Lauren breathed as she looked at Cedar Creek Camp. She was stroking Twilight's neck in delight. Most of the time, Twilight looked just like any other ordinary grey pony, but when Lauren said the words of the Turning Spell he changed into a beautiful white unicorn who could talk, do magic and fly. One of his magic powers meant that when he touched his horn to a rock of rose quartz he could see anything he wanted, anywhere in the world.

'That's where we'll be tomorrow night,' Twilight said, gazing into the rock.

Lauren nodded. She and Twilight were going to the camp for six days. Mel, Lauren's best friend, was going too, with her pony, Shadow. 'It's going to be so cool,' Lauren told Twilight happily. 'We get to showjump and do cross-country and go for rides in the woods and there's all the other stuff like camp fires and swimming in the creek.'

'I'm really looking forward to meeting the other ponies,' Twilight said.

'Yeah,' agreed Lauren. 'And all the

new people. I wonder who Mel and I will be sharing our cabin with.'

'Only a few hours till we find out,' Twilight said excitedly.

Reluctantly, Lauren pulled her eyes away from the image in front of her. 'I think we should go home now. We're going to have to be up early in the morning.'

Twilight nodded. As he took his
horn away from the rock, the picture
faded. Lauren climbed on to his warm
back. Cantering forward, Twilight
plunged into the sky. As they swooped
through the trees, Lauren's long fair hair
whipped back from her face. Excitement
buzzed through her as she thought
about the next day. What was riding
camp going to be like? She couldn't
wait to find out!

'Look, girls!' Mrs Cassidy, Mel's mum,
said the next day as, they drove towards
a large white sign saying:

*CEDAR CREEK CAMP THIS WAY!*

'Hurray!' Mel cried. 'We're here!'

Mrs Cassidy turned in to a bumpy
track that led into the woods.

'I wish Jess was with us,' Lauren said
to Mel.

'We'll tell her all about it,' Mel
replied. Jessica was their other best
friend. She hadn't been able to come to

camp because she was going on holiday with her family.

Lauren nodded and then caught sight of water glinting through the trees. 'Look!'

'I wonder if that's Cedar Creek,' Mel said. 'You know, the creek that gave Cedar Creek Camp its name.'

'It is,' Lauren replied, remembering the magic images she'd seen the night before. 'It runs all the way through the woods up to the campsite.' She saw Mel look at her in surprise, and hastily added, 'I . . . I saw it on the map on the website.'

Mel grinned. 'I've been looking at the website a lot too. Last night, I was looking at the photos. I kept imagining being here.'

*Phew*, Lauren thought. Sometimes it was very hard to remember to keep Twilight's magic a secret from her family and friends!

The car and trailer bumped along the uneven track until they reached an open wooden gate. As Mrs Cassidy drove through it, Lauren could see Cedar Creek Riding Camp spread out before them. It looked just like it had when she and Twilight had seen it the night before, only it wasn't quiet and deserted any more: there were people and ponies everywhere!

Mrs Cassidy found a space near the barn and stopped the car. Lauren and Mel had the doors open before she'd

even switched off the engine. Girls and
their parents were unloading ponies from
trailers all around them and lugging
great heavy trunks and armfuls of tack
across the field towards the barn.

'Look, that's where we'll be sleeping,'
Mel said, pointing to the three white
cabins nearby. They each had a small
porch and cheerful window boxes,
spilling over with pink and purple
flowers.

'I wonder which cabin we'll be in,'
Lauren said, watching a couple of girls
carrying rucksacks into the middle
cabin.

Just then, a woman bustled up to
them. She was wearing navy jodhpurs

and a smart white polo shirt with the Cedar Creek logo — a black horse trotting through cedar trees — on the front. Her shoulder-length brown hair, slightly streaked with grey, was tucked behind her ears and she was holding a clipboard.

'Hello,' she said, smiling. 'And who might you two be?'

'Lauren Foster and Mel Cassidy,' replied Lauren.

'Pleased to meet you,' the woman said, ticking their names off on her list. 'I'm Hilary. I own Cedar Creek and I'm the senior instructor and counsellor. I hope you'll have a great stay with us.'

Lauren thought she was going to like

Hilary. She had a no-nonsense air about her, but her smile was friendly.

As Mrs Cassidy came over to introduce herself, Lauren and Mel looked around.

'I wonder what we do now,' Mel said to Lauren.

Hilary overheard. 'First you need to get your ponies settled into their stalls.' She checked her list. 'Twilight and Shadow, isn't it?'

Mel and Lauren nodded.

'They're next door to each other in stalls seven and eight in the barn,' Hilary went on. 'When you've got them sorted you can start moving into your cabins.' She checked her clipboard again.

'Lauren, you'll be in the Owls cabin, which is the furthest on the right. Mel, you'll be in the Bluejays cabin, which is next door.'

Lauren blinked. For a moment, she wondered if she'd heard properly. *Next door!*

'But we can't be in different cabins!' Mel exclaimed.

'We wanted to be in the same cabin!' Lauren protested. She and Mel had been planning on spending every moment at camp together.

Hilary looked at them sympathetically. 'Sorry, girls, but we have a policy here at Cedar Creek that campers should share with people they haven't arrived with.

We find it makes everyone mix much better. After all, part of the fun in coming to camp is meeting new people.' She smiled cheerfully. 'OK, I'll leave you to get sorted out. See you later.'

As she strode off, Lauren and Mel looked at each other in dismay.

# Two

Mel turned to Mrs Cassidy. 'Mum! Lauren and I have *got* to share a cabin!'

'Don't make a fuss, Mel,' Mrs Cassidy said. 'You heard what Hilary said and she's right. It will be a good way for you to make new friends.'

Mel's eyes filled with tears. 'But, Mum, we really want to be together. It

won't be nearly so much fun if we're in
different cabins. Please talk to Hilary.
Please!'

'I'm sorry, Mel,' Mrs Cassidy replied,
'but it's obviously a camp rule.'

Lauren swallowed. 'I suppose it won't
be that bad, Mel,' she said, feeling upset
but trying very hard to make the best of
it. 'After all, it's only for sleeping. We'll
be with each other the rest of the time.'

Mel didn't look convinced.

Shadow whinnied impatiently from
inside the trailer.

'I think Shadow's trying to tell us
something,' Mrs Cassidy said. 'Come on,
you two, stop looking so miserable and
let's get those ponies out!'

★

Lauren and Mel settled Twilight and
Shadow into the barn. It had a wide
central aisle with nine stalls on either
side. At the far end was a large tack
room. Ponies were being put into stalls
and people were unloading their tack.
The air was full of excited chatter and
girls calling out to each other.

'Erin! Hi! Come and see my new
pony!'

'Paige! You've had your hair cut!'

'Hey, Natasha, do you think we'll go
riding bareback again this year?'

Lauren led Twilight into his stall. The
excitement she'd felt when they had
first arrived had fizzled out. She
couldn't believe she and Mel were
going to be in different cabins. They'd
planned on having midnight feasts and
telling ghost stories every night. Now
they wouldn't be able to do any of
those things. As she began to take off
the travelling wraps that had protected
Twilight's legs on the journey, she told
him all about it.

'I really wish we were in the same cabin,' she finished sadly.

Twilight nuzzled her sympathetically.

Lauren gave him a hug. 'I'll come and talk to you later,' she said. 'I'd better go and unpack my things now.'

She and Mel headed back across the busy campsite to the car.

'Goodbye, girls,' Mrs Cassidy said as they heaved their rucksacks out of the car. 'Have a great time. I'll see you on Friday.'

They waved her off, then began to lug their rucksacks across the grass. All around them, other girls were saying goodbye to their parents too and heading towards the cabins. As they got closer to the three cabins, Mel's steps got slower.

'Come on,' Lauren said reassuringly.
'It's not going to be that bad.' Looking at
her cabin, she hoped she was right!

As she pushed open the door, she saw
that the cabin had three bunk beds and
one single bed. Each bunk had a name
label on the end of it. There was a stripy
red rug on the floor and bright gingham
curtains at the window. Four girls, all
about Lauren's age, were sitting on one
of the bottom bunks. They were all
laughing together, but they broke off as
Lauren came in.

'Hi,' Lauren said, feeling awkward as
they all looked at her.

A small skinny girl with short fair

hair stood up. 'Hello,' she said. 'I'm
Natasha. Are you Lauren?'

'Yes,' Lauren replied, relieved to see that
Natasha smiled at her in a friendly way.

'We were wondering when you'd get
here,' a girl with shoulder-length dark
blonde hair said. 'We saw your name on
your bunk bed. I'm Rose and this is
Julia.' She tilted her head towards a girl
with a long red plait.

'Hi,' Julia said shyly. Her voice was
hardly louder than a whisper and she
blushed as if embarrassed to be
speaking out loud. 'I'm sharing this
bunk with Rose.'

'And I'm sharing the bunk by the
window with Natasha,' said the girl

sitting on the other side of Julia. She
bounced up. She was tall and slim with
wavy brown hair and sensible brown
eyes. 'My name's Jasmine. Is this your
first time at Cedar Creek, Lauren?'

Lauren nodded.

'Mine too,' Jasmine grinned. 'But it
seems cool. I don't have a pony of my
own,' she went on. 'I'm borrowing one

called Nugget from Hilary for the week.
Mum and Dad say that they might buy
me my own pony if I get on OK here.'

'I came here last year,' Natasha
explained to Lauren. 'Julia was here then
too. It was great!'

Julia nodded. 'Hilary and the other
instructors are really nice,' she said quietly.

That's your bed over there, Lauren.'
Natasha pointed to a bunk bed in the
corner.

'Thanks,' Lauren replied. She walked
over to it and looked eagerly to see the
name of the person she'd be sharing it
with. But there was only a single label
saying *Lauren Foster* on the bed.

Jasmine saw her looking at the label.

'There's no one sharing with you,' she explained. 'Hope – she's the counsellor for this cabin – told us that a girl called Ellen was supposed to be staying in here with us but she got chickenpox and hasn't been able to come.'

'Oh,' Lauren said, feeling disappointed that she didn't have anyone to share with. She looked at the single bed in the opposite corner. 'Is that Hope's bed, then?'

'Yes,' Natasha replied. 'She's gone to check on her horse. She said he's got a sore foot.'

'She told us to unpack,' Jasmine put in. 'I think we should get a move on. She'll be back soon.'

Natasha nodded. 'You have to finish telling us about the show, Rose.'

Jasmine and Julia giggled, remembering what they'd been talking about when Lauren arrived.

'I can't believe you fell off twice,' Jasmine said, opening her rucksack.

Rose grinned. 'I told you. I was useless! There I was sitting in the saddle and it was like, *where's his head?*' She and the others started to laugh.

'What happened?' Lauren asked, keen to join in.

Rose shook her head. 'Oh, nothing important. It's just a silly story I was telling the others about the first show I took my pony Sinbad to.'

'Very silly,' Jasmine giggled.

Natasha began to pull things out of her rucksack. 'Falling off over his tail!' she grinned, glancing at Rose. 'Even *I've* never done that.'

Unable to join in, Lauren went over to her bunk bed and put her rucksack down. The others gradually stopped giggling and began to unpack too. Jasmine was asking Natasha about camp and Rose was talking quietly to Julia as they finished putting their things away in the small cupboards beside their bunks. Wishing she had someone to share her bunk with and talk to, Lauren glanced at the empty bunk above her. *If only Mel was here*, she thought longingly.

She thought about the next-door cabin. What was Mel doing? Was she thinking about her too?

The door opened and a girl of about eighteen came in. Her brown hair was pulled back from her cheerful face in a stubby ponytail. Seeing Lauren, she smiled. 'Hi, you must be Lauren Foster. I'm Hope, the counsellor for this cabin.'

'Hi,' Lauren said.

'If you need anything at all, just ask me,' Hope told her cheerfully. 'Now, you lot, are you all just about ready?' she asked, looking around. 'Hilary wants everyone to come to the recreation room before dinner for the welcome meeting.'

After putting the last of their things

away, the Owls followed Hope to the
long, low building in the centre of the
camp. One side was the dining-hall and
the other was the recreation room
where the campers could go during free
time. There were old brown sofas in it, a
ping-pong table at one end of the
room, a TV and a craft table.

The other campers and counsellors
were all there. Lauren saw Mel sitting on
a sofa with five other girls. *They must be
the Bluejays*, Lauren thought.

She wanted to go and sit with Mel
but there wasn't any room on that sofa,
so she went with her cabin and sat down
on the sofa opposite. Mel looked much
happier than she had when Lauren had

left her at the Bluejays door. A girl with red shoulder-length curls was sitting next to her. She had dancing green eyes and a mischievous smile. Glancing across the room, the red-headed girl whispered something to Mel. Lauren saw Mel giggle at her and grin.

Lauren felt a flicker of jealousy but she squashed it down and tried to feel pleased that Mel was making friends. She wondered if the red-headed girl and Mel were bunkmates.

Just then, Hilary clapped her hands. 'OK, guys, listen up! I won't keep you for long – I imagine you're probably starving – but I just want to introduce everyone, give out the schedules and run

through some camp rules. First of all,
the introductions. As you all know, I'm
Hilary, the senior instructor. Your other
two instructors will be Tom, who's my
son –' she pointed to a young man who
looked about twenty – 'and Emily, who
is a graduate of the camp and is training
to be a riding instructor. Then there are
your cabin counsellors – Hope, Andrea
and Meagan – and our wonderful cook,
Karen.' A large lady wearing a white
apron smiled round at them. 'Any
problems, come and find any of us. Now,
on to the schedules,' Hilary started to
give out some sheets of paper. 'At Cedar
Creek we ride every morning, and then
we have an unmounted session after

lunch where we do things without the
ponies – demonstrations and lessons on
stable management, things like that. Then
we have a fun riding session in the
afternoon. We expect you to be up by
seven-thirty to help with mucking out
and grooming, breakfast is at nine and
lessons start at ten after you've done
your camp chores.'

The red-headed girl who'd been
giggling with Mel stuck up her hand.
'What are camp chores?'

'Well, Kate, every day each cabin is
given a chore to do – either sweeping
the yard or cleaning up the tack room
or something like that,' Hilary explained.
She smiled. 'I know it might sound like

a lot of work but don't worry. We just like you all to have some responsibility for keeping the camp neat and tidy. It's also part of the team competition.'

'Competition?' asked Jasmine.

'Yes, we have a competition for the best cabin. All week you have the chance to earn points in your cabin teams,' Hilary replied. 'You can get points in mounted competitions, for doing your chores, for keeping your cabins tidy and for the turnout of you and your pony at the start of each day. At the end of the week the team with the most points will win a trophy each.'

Lauren glanced at Mel. The competition sounded fun but it would have been even better if she and Mel had been in the same team.

'And just so you know,' Hilary went on, 'your free time is your own, but we do ask that campers don't go into each other's cabins after dinner and, from that time in the evening, the stables are also out of bounds.

'Out of bounds!' The words burst out of Lauren before she could stop them.

Hilary nodded. 'Yes, we've found that ponies don't appreciate late-night gossip and midnight feasts as much as their riders!' She looked round at them all. 'It's my guess that you lot would be in the barn all night if you were allowed to, but the ponies really do need time to

sleep and relax, so no going into the
barn after dinner, OK?'

The other campers nodded but Lauren
was too stunned to respond. Her thoughts
were reeling. If the barn was out of
bounds then she couldn't go and see
Twilight at night; that meant no talking –
and no flying – for a whole week!

CHAPTER

# Three

When Hilary had finished her talk, the campers headed into the dining-hall for dinner. Lauren followed the other Owls, but her mind was on Twilight. She'd never imagined that the stables would be out of bounds. *Maybe no one will notice if I sneak out there*, she thought hopefully.

The dining-hall was laid out with five

tables covered with cheerful checked
tablecloths. Along one side there was a
counter set out with an enormous dish
of macaroni cheese, huge platters of hot
dogs and a salad bar. Everyone crowded
around the food table, laughing and
talking. Lauren helped herself and then
went looking for Mel.

She found her sitting at a table by the
window with three of the other
Bluejays. There was still some space at
the table and Lauren headed over. The
Bluejays were flicking bread at each
other with their fingers.

'Got you, Erin!' Kate shouted as a piece
of bread bounced off the spiky-haired
girl's nose.

Erin grinned and flicked a piece back. It missed and flew over Kate's shoulder, landing on the Eagles' table. They looked round mystified and the Bluejays burst out laughing.

'Hi!' Lauren said, raising her voice to speak above the scraping of chairs on the floor and the noisy chattering of the dining-hall.

Kate looked her up and down. 'Who are you?' she said in a not-altogether friendly way.

'This is Lauren, my best friend from home,' Mel said. 'Lauren, this is Kate – who I'm sharing a bunk with, Erin and Paige,' she added nodding to a quieter girl with a blonde ponytail

and the girl with the spiky hair.

Paige smiled but Kate and Erin didn't.

'Sit down, Lauren,' urged Mel.

But before Lauren could, a girl came over from the serving area.

'Hey, Allison, come and sit with us!' Kate called, pointing to the seat beside Mel.

'Thanks,' said the girl as she sat down. She grinned. 'So we've got ourselves a Bluejays table.'

Mel looked as if she didn't know what to do. Lauren gave a shrug. 'It's OK,' she said quietly to Mel. 'I should probably go and sit with the rest of my cabin.' She tried to sound like she didn't care, but she did – she cared a lot. She hoped Mel would offer to come with her but she didn't.

Feeling a bit hurt, Lauren went over to where the Owls were sitting. As she sat down, she glanced round. Mel was trying to take an enormous bite of her hot dog and giggling as Kate tickled her at the same time. Lauren looked at her meal. Suddenly she didn't feel quite so hungry any more.

All through dinner, Lauren heard giggles coming from the Bluejays' table and soon bits of bread were flying round the room, until Emily noticed and told them to clear it all up. Lauren tried to be glad that Mel was getting on so well with her cabinmates, but it was hard. *She* wanted to be having fun with Mel. Next to her, Julia was busy talking to Natasha and across the table, Jasmine was talking to Rose. Lauren suppressed a sigh and ate in silence.

After dinner was over and the plates had been cleared away, the Bluejays went through to the recreation room and started playing a noisy game of snap. It looked like fun. *I suppose I could always go and ask if I could play too*, Lauren thought as she went into the room.

'Hi,' Mel greeted her as she walked over.

'Snap! I won!' Erin shouted, scooping up all the cards. 'New game!'

'Can I play?' Lauren asked.

Kate jumped to her feet. 'Sorry, but we're done playing now. We're going back to the cabin – we need to talk tactics for the team cup. We are *so* going to win it!'

The others grinned and began to stand up too.

Lauren looked at Mel. 'Are you going too?'

Mel looked awkward. 'Um –'

'What are you waiting for, Mel?' Kate interrupted her. 'See you tomorrow, Lisa.'

'Lauren,' Lauren corrected her. 'My name's Lauren.'

Kate shrugged as if it didn't matter. 'Come on, Mel.'

Mel got to her feet. 'I'll see you tomorrow, OK?' she said to Lauren.

Lauren nodded. Her throat felt tight.

Mel went off with the others.

A great wave of homesickness suddenly swept over Lauren and, biting her lip, she hurried out of the door.

She ran across the grass towards her cabin. The barn loomed in the distance. As she looked at it, she suddenly wanted to talk to Twilight. *No one will notice*, she thought. *They're all busy.* Changing direction she ran towards the barn.

She reached it without anyone seeing her and opened the doors just enough to slip inside. Hay nets were hanging outside the stalls for the morning and there was no sound apart from the occasional snort and stamp of a hoof.

'Twilight!' Lauren whispered.

From his stall near the tack room, Twilight gave a welcoming snicker.

Lauren ran down the aisle and slid the bolts on his door across. Stepping into the warm stall, she put her arms around his smooth neck. 'Oh, Twilight, I'm glad to see you,' she told him. 'I'm feeling really lonely and I badly wanted to talk to you. But I can't stay long. I'm not supposed to be here.' She said the words of the Turning Spell.

> '*Twilight Star, Twilight Star,*
> *Twinkling high above so far.*
> *Shining light, shining bright,*
> *Will you grant my wish tonight?*
> *Let my little horse forlorn*
> *Be at last a unicorn!*'

A bright purple flash lit up the dark barn and Twilight turned into a unicorn. His

grey coat suddenly gleamed snow-white
and his mane and tail shone silver.

'What do you mean, you're not
supposed to be here?' he asked in surprise.

Lauren explained about the camp rule.
'The barn is out of bounds after dinner,
which means I'm not going to be able

to come here at night unless I sneak out, and just hope no one sees me.'

'That sounds a bit risky.' Twilight looked worried.

Lauren nodded. 'I don't know what to do. It'll be really weird not turning you into a unicorn all week.'

'No magic for a whole week,' Twilight said slowly.

They stared at each other.

'I suppose there'll be lots of other things to do,' Lauren said, stroking him.

Twilight nodded. 'You shouldn't risk it. If you get caught here, you'll get in trouble and . . .'

Suddenly he stiffened and broke off. 'Lauren, I think I just heard something outside!' He looked towards the door. His horn started to glow as he used his magic powers to make his hearing extra-sensitive. 'Yes! There's definitely someone coming!'

Lauren gabbled out the words of the Undoing Spell and, in an instant, Twilight changed back. Lauren ran out of the stall cursing herself for leaving the barn door open. Could she get out of the barn without being discovered?

The beam of a torch swung round the aisle.

She was too late.

'Who's there?' a voice asked sharply.

Lauren froze. It was Hilary!

# CHAPTER
# Four

The torch caught Lauren in its beam.

'What are you doing in here?' Hilary asked, coming down the aisle.

Lauren's cheeks felt like they were on fire. 'I . . . I just wanted to see Twilight,' she whispered, wishing she was somewhere – *anywhere* – else.

There was a moment's silence and

then Hilary sighed and her voice
softened. 'It's your first time at camp,
isn't it, Lauren? Were you feeling
homesick?'

Lauren nodded.

'It happens to a lot of people on the
first night. You'll soon settle in,' Hilary
said gently. 'But you *must* obey the camp
rules. We really can't have campers in the
barn at night without adult supervision.
Now, seeing as it's the first night, let's
just forget I ever found you here. But,'
she added warningly, 'it really mustn't
happen again. If it does, I'm afraid I'll
have no choice but to send you home. I
can't have campers deliberately breaking
the rules. Do you understand?'

'I understand,' Lauren replied.

Hilary smiled. 'Good girl. Say goodnight to Twilight and run on back to your cabin before the bedtime bell goes.'

Lauren got back to the Owls' cabin

just as the bell began to ring. The others
looked at her curiously.

'Where have you been?' Natasha
asked.

'Just around,' Lauren said vaguely.

She went to the tiny bathroom,
brushed her teeth and got changed into
her pyjamas. It felt strange climbing
into the unfamiliar bunk beds. As Hope
said goodnight and turned off the light,
she heard the creaks of the others
shifting in their beds and the quiet
sound of their breathing as they
gradually fell asleep.

Lauren stared at the bed above her
and thought about Mel next door. Was
she having trouble sleeping too? This

just wasn't how she'd imagined her first night at camp would be at all!

'Come on, guys, you've got to get them cleaner than that!' Kate's voice rang out across the grooming area the next morning, as she bossed the other Bluejays around. 'We want to get loads of points in the grooming inspection so that we can win the cup.'

Brushing out the tangles in Twilight's tail, Lauren frowned. They'd only been up an hour and already Kate was annoying her. While the Owls and the Eagles were grooming quietly, Kate was charging about, noisily organizing the Bluejays. Lauren had hardly had a chance to speak to Mel because Mel had been far too busy trying to get Shadow's coat clean enough to meet with Kate's approval.

Rose came up to Natasha, who was standing near Lauren. 'Kate's a bit bossy, isn't she?' she said in a low voice.

'You can say that again,' Natasha muttered back.

'She's acting like it's a show or something,' Rose said, watching as Kate carefully removed a remaining speck of dirt from her pony's coat with a damp cloth and then put some spray on his mane to make it lie perfectly flat. 'We're only having a lesson.'

But when the time came for Hilary,

Tom and Emily to inspect the ponies before the lesson, it became obvious that Kate's bossiness had paid off. The Bluejays' ponies looked spotlessly clean and the team marks reflected it.

'Eagles, we've given you six marks. Owls, you got seven and the Bluejays did exceptionally well, you get ten out of ten,' Hilary announced.

Kate whooped, causing several ponies to jump in alarm.

'And for the cabin inspection this morning,' Hilary went on checking her sheet. 'Bluejays get ten out of ten again, Eagles seven and Owls six.'

All the Bluejays cheered.

Hilary clapped her hands for

attention. 'OK, Owls you'll be with me for a riding lesson. Bluejays and Eagles, you'll be doing showjumping with Tom and Emily.'

As the showjumping groups left the arena to ride into the field, Lauren gathered up her reins.

'Are you ready, everyone?' Hilary

called out to the Owls. 'Prepare to walk
. . . and walk on.'

Lauren and Twilight set off, and
Lauren hoped that the first riding lesson
would be more fun than the chores had
been.

Despite not being with Mel, Lauren
really enjoyed the lesson. She didn't have
riding lessons at home and Hilary was a
good teacher. She explained things
clearly and was quick to praise any
improvement in the campers' riding.
Lauren learnt how to leg yield, which
meant getting the pony to step sideways
but forward at the same time so they
moved diagonally across the ring. At first

she could only get Twilight to take a couple of steps but by the end of the lesson he was going all the way from the centre of the arena to the outside.

'Great work, Lauren,' Hilary praised her. 'I can see you're a fast learner!'

Lauren blushed but her heart leapt. She patted Twilight's neck. 'Good boy,' she said.

After the lesson, they put the ponies out in the fields. Twilight and Shadow were sharing a paddock with Rose's pony, Sinbad, and Nugget, the pony that Jasmine was borrowing for camp.

'Hi!' Mel called to Lauren as she led Shadow to the paddock. 'We had a great lesson!' she said excitedly. 'We did lots of jumping. How about you? Your lesson didn't look as much fun as ours.'

'Well, it was! It was really good!' Lauren knew she sounded crabby but she couldn't help feeling hurt that Mel had hardly said a single word to her that morning.

Mel shot her a surprised look. 'What's up with you?'

'Nothing,' Lauren sighed. 'Sorry, I didn't mean to snap. I'm just hungry.'

'Me too,' agreed Mel. 'Let's go and get some lunch.'

After putting the ponies out, they got changed into shorts and went to the dining-hall. There was a salad bar set up again and a make-your-own sandwich table. Lauren and Mel made a pile of peanut butter sandwiches and cream cheese and ham bagels, and then filled their trays up with crisps, apples and a huge glass each of chilled lemonade.

They went to sit outside together. As they talked about their lessons, Lauren felt the tension that had been building up inside her slowly fade away. This was how she'd imagined camp to be – she and Mel having a great time and talking about their favourite thing – horses!

'So what are the other Owls like?' Mel asked.

'OK,' Lauren replied. 'Pretty quiet.'

'The other Bluejays are *definitely* not

quiet!' Mel grinned. 'We had a huge
pillow fight last night and tonight Kate
wants us to tell ghost stories!'

Lauren felt a stab of jealousy. She and
Mel had planned to tell ghost stories at
night. But that was when they'd thought
they'd be sharing a cabin.

'Kate's really good fun,' Mel enthused.

'She seems a bit bossy,' Lauren said
shortly.

'A bit,' Mel said. 'But she's really cool
*and* she's a brilliant rider.'

Lauren didn't want to spend
lunchtime listening to Mel talking about
how great Kate was. She quickly
changed the subject. 'Shall we go to the
creek when we've finished eating?'

Mel nodded. 'Yeah! We should have
time before the unmounted session.
What's your team doing this afternoon?'

'Getting a pony ready for a show,'
Lauren replied. 'How about you?'

'We've got a talk on Western tack,'
Mel replied.

Lauren sighed. 'I wish we were in the
same team and we could go to things
together.'

'I know,' Mel said, 'but at least
everyone else is really fun.'

*Everyone in your cabin*, Lauren thought.
It wasn't that she disliked the other
Owls, but they didn't seem to have as
much fun as the Bluejays.

Mel got to her feet. 'Come on, I'm

finished. Let's dump our plates and go to the creek.'

Lauren jumped to her feet and followed her across the grass.

Lauren and Mel had fun paddling in the creek. There were seven other

campers there too, mainly from the Eagles' cabin, and Meagan and Emily were supervising.

When it was almost time for the afternoon sessions to start, Lauren and Mel headed back to the barn. As they reached it, Kate came running out from behind it, chasing Erin and Allison across the grass with a wet sponge in each hand. She chucked the sponges and they splattered against Erin and Allison's shorts. 'Yuck!' Allison exclaimed, chucking the sponge back. Kate ducked, laughing.

'Hey, Mel!' she shouted. 'Where have you been? We've been having a water fight. Now we're going to go to the hay

barn before the Western thing. There's a
rope hanging from the ceiling and you
can swing on it. Want to come? We've
got ten minutes before the
demonstration.'

'Sure!' Mel replied. She turned to
Lauren. 'Come on.'

Lauren hesitated. She wasn't sure
Kate's invitation had included her.

'The Owls are all in the main barn
if you're looking for them, Lauren,' Kate
called out.

*Guess I was right*, Lauren thought. *She
didn't want me to come!*

'Come on, Mel. You can see Lauren
later,' Kate shouted.

Mel looked at Lauren. 'Um . . .'

*Please Mel, don't go with them*, Lauren thought.

'I'd better go with the others. See you later, Lauren,' Mel said, and she hurried off towards the other Bluejays. 'Wait for me, Kate! I'm coming!'

Lauren stood and stared. How *could* Mel have gone off like that? It was bad enough that they were separated in the evenings and for the lessons and demonstrations without Mel going off at other times too.

She watched as Mel ran into the hay barn with the other Bluejays.

'Thanks, Mel,' Lauren muttered. 'Thanks a lot!'

# Five

After the unmounted demonstrations, everyone went on a trail ride. Despite still feeling hurt about Mel going off with Kate at lunchtime, Lauren hoped they would finally get to ride together. But some of the ponies weren't used to being in the woods so Hilary explained that she wanted to team the nervous ponies with the steady ones.

'Lauren, Twilight seems very calm.
Would you mind riding with Rose,
please?' Hilary said as she organized
everyone into pairs. 'Sinbad isn't used to
being in the woods, is he, Rose?'

'No,' Rose replied, 'he gets a bit
nervous riding through trees.'

'Well, I'm sure Twilight will help steady him,' Hilary said. 'He seems a very sensible sort of pony.'

She smiled at Lauren. Lauren forced a smile back.

When everyone was sorted into pairs, the ride set off. There were a lot of them but it was fun trotting and cantering through the woods together.

At first Sinbad – Rose's young dapple-grey pony – was nervous, looking round at everything with wide eyes and shying at tree stumps and branches that cracked underfoot on the sandy trails. But Twilight kept touching him with his nose in a reassuring way and gradually Sinbad started to relax.

'He really likes Twilight,' Rose said to Lauren when they slowed to a walk.

Lauren smiled at her. She liked Rose. 'How long have you had Sinbad?'

'Two years. How about you and Twilight?'

'Just one year,' Lauren replied.

She was about to ask Rose more about Sinbad when Hilary gave the instruction to trot on again, and they had to concentrate on their riding. They were out for almost two hours in the shade of the trees. Afterwards they cooled the ponies down in the creek and then turned them out in the paddocks. Then they set to work cleaning their tack.

Mel went and sat with the other Bluejays right away. Lauren hesitated and took her tack over to where the Owls were sitting.

*I'll talk to her when we finish*, Lauren thought, glancing across at her best friend. *We can do something together before dinner.*

'Are you OK?'

Lauren looked round. It was Jasmine who'd spoken.

'Umm . . . yes,' Lauren replied.

'It's just you seem quiet,' Jasmine said. She looked in the direction of the Bluejays. 'Is it because your friend Mel is over there?'

Lauren nodded.

'It must be weird – having your best friend here and not being in the same cabin,' Jasmine said sympathetically. She looked at the others. 'Look, why don't we all go into the woods when we've finished and practise for this quiz.' Lauren remembered that there was going to be a team pony quiz after dinner that night. 'There are some tree stumps we can sit on and we can take some stable management books with us,' Jasmine went on.

'OK,' Rose agreed. Natasha and Julia nodded.

Lauren hesitated. She wanted to go but if she did, she wouldn't be able to see Mel. 'Thanks but I don't think I

will,' she told them. She saw their looks
of surprise. 'I was going to meet up
with Mel,' she said by way of an excuse.

Jasmine shrugged. 'OK.' She turned
back to cleaning her bridle and didn't
say anything more.

Lauren felt bad. She knew Jasmine
had just been trying to be friendly. She
finished her tack and then went over to
the Bluejays. They looked up as she
approached. Lauren felt awkward. 'Um,
hi, Mel,' she said, feeling very aware they
were all listening. 'When . . . when
you've finished your tack, do you want
to come back to my cabin? I thought
we could look at some books before this
quiz tonight.'

Mel frowned. 'Um, that would be
good but –'

'She can't,' Kate interrupted. 'Sorry,
but we're having a team meeting. *Just* for
the Bluejays,' she added.

'Oh.' Lauren glanced at Mel.

Mel shrugged awkwardly. 'Sorry, Lauren. I'll see you later, OK?'

Lauren swallowed. 'Yep,' she muttered. 'OK.'

Feeling her eyes suddenly start to fill, she swung round. She wasn't going to cry in front of them. She wasn't!

She looked round to where the other Owls had been but Jasmine, Natasha, Julia and Rose had already left to go to the woods. Lauren wondered if she should catch up with them. But what would she say? Looking around, she felt suddenly very alone.

She ran down to the paddocks. Hearing her coming, Twilight whinnied in greeting and trotted over to the gate.

Lauren put her arms around him.
'Oh, Twilight,' she whispered, her heart
feeling like a lead weight in her chest.
'I never thought camp was going to be
like this!'

Although Lauren was feeling low, the
pony quiz that evening turned out to be
much more fun than she had expected.
She had always found it easy to
remember pony things, and Natasha,
Rose, Jasmine and Julia knew a lot too.
Hilary called out questions. The person
who got the answer right first won their
team a chance to answer three more
questions and get more points. The
Owls' hands were the first up for nearly

every question. Lauren got so involved
in it that she forgot to think about Mel
at all. It was really good fun coming
up with the answers for the team
questions with the other Owls, especially
since they got so many answers right!
They won the quiz easily and were
given a bag of sweets to share and six
points towards their team-cup total.

'That was brilliant!' Rose exclaimed as
they shared the sweets out. 'I can't
believe we did so well.'

'You answered loads of questions,
Lauren,' Jasmine put in.

'And you didn't even practise with us,'
Natasha said.

Lauren thought about two questions

she'd got wrong and felt slightly guilty. 'I should have done,' she said, meaning it. 'Then I might not have messed up those two questions.'

'It wouldn't have made any difference,' Rose told her. 'And you got more starter questions right than the rest of us.'

Lauren grinned at her happily.

'We're only one point behind the Bluejays now!' Natasha exclaimed. 'We *must* do well in the pony inspection tomorrow.'

They all agreed, and going to bed that night Lauren realized that she felt happier than she had done all camp. She set her alarm clock for six-thirty.

Twilight was going to look spotless the next morning!

When Lauren's alarm clock rang, she jumped out of bed. She and the others went to the barn and set to work washing tails and grooming until their ponies shone. Kate looked very surprised to see them all there when she and the rest of the Bluejays came to the barn at seven o'clock. She scowled when she saw how clean the Owls' ponies were looking. Lauren hid a grin. The Owls were going to get as many points as the Bluejays that morning, she was sure of it!

After breakfast, they got changed into

their riding clothes and then went back to tack up.

As Lauren finished doing up Twilight's girth, she stood back to admire him. But as she did so, her foot bumped into a bucket of dirty water that had been put down just behind her. It overturned with a clatter and splashed everywhere, dirty droplets of water splattering Lauren's cream jodhpurs and soaking Twilight's front legs.

Lauren gasped in horror.

'Oh, Lauren!' Rose exclaimed. 'Why didn't you clear that bucket away?'

'I didn't leave it there!' Lauren said.

Hearing a snort of laughter, she swung round. Kate and Erin were giggling. 'What a pity. You won't get full marks for your turnout now,' Kate said.

Lauren shot her a furious look. 'Did you put that bucket there?'

'No,' Kate said quickly. But her eyes danced mischievously.

Lauren glanced at Mel but she was talking to Paige at the other end of the horse line and hadn't noticed.

'Quick, Lauren!' Jasmine urged. 'You'd better get on. Hilary, Tom and Emily are coming!'

Lauren brushed away the water as best she could and mounted. After all her hard work, it wasn't fair! Now her team would lose points. She just knew Kate had put the bucket there.

To her relief, Hilary only knocked two points off their total. 'I can see it must have been an accident,' she said. 'The rest of Twilight is beautifully groomed, Lauren.'

Kate looked disappointed.

'So that's ten out of ten for the Bluejays, eight for the Owls and six for the Eagles,' Hilary announced, checking her clipboard. 'If you can get into your rides, please. Eagles with me, Owls with Tom and Bluejays with Emily.'

The jumping lesson was really fun. Tom put out a line of low jumps. All five ponies jumped very well, so Tom made the girls take their stirrups away.

'Well done,' he said as they completed the jumps. 'Let's try jumping a bit higher now.'

He dragged a jump to the centre of the field and raised the bar.

'That looks big,' Jasmine said nervously.

'Who'll go first?' Tom asked.

'I will,' Lauren offered.

Twilight jumped the new fence easily, as did all the other ponies apart from Nugget. The first time he jumped it OK, but after that he started refusing. Jasmine looked anxious, and she was sitting stiffly in the saddle. 'You have to relax,' Tom told her. 'Nugget can jump it easily.'

Jasmine got Nugget over the jump one more time, but as he landed he threw up his head and after that he refused the fence every single time. She began to look very frustrated. Tom walked over to help her. 'Get off and give your ponies a rest for a few minutes,' he told the others.

As Lauren dismounted, she looked across to the other end of the jumping field where the Bluejays were jumping a bright-red wall with pots of white flowers beside it. Lauren wondered how Shadow would cope. Until recently he had been very scared of jumping. Lauren and Twilight had visited him at night and helped him overcome his fear. But

he still didn't like jumping unusual
fences. Lauren led Twilight over to
watch.

Shadow refused the wall the first time
he reached it.

'He hasn't jumped a wall like this before,' Mel explained to Emily.

'Why don't you take him up to it, Mel?' Kate called out from where she was sitting on her black pony, Chess. 'Circle it a few times so he can have a good look.'

'Thank you, Kate,' Emily commented dryly. 'I'm quite capable of taking the lesson.'

Kate grinned at her. 'Sorry, Em!'

'Still, what you said was good advice,' Emily agreed. 'Mel, why don't you do what Kate suggested?'

Mel let Shadow have a good look at the wall and then circled round it. When he was cantering smoothly and calmly she turned towards it. He flew over it easily.

'Good boy!' Mel exclaimed. She rode back to the line. Kate grinned at her and leant over Chess's neck. She seemed to be giving Mel more advice. Mel nodded eagerly.

Lauren's stomach clenched. She was the one Mel usually turned to for advice! She quickly turned Twilight away.

'Hi, Lauren,' Mel said, catching up with her after the lesson. 'Want to go and get some lunch?'

Lauren nodded briefly. She was in a bad mood. She couldn't stop thinking

about the way Mel had listened so
eagerly to Kate during the lesson.

As they headed to the dining-hall,
Mel sighed happily. 'We had a really
good lesson. Kate gave me some really
useful tips for jumping Shadow. She just
knew exactly what to do. She's brilliant!'

Hurt surged through Lauren. Mel
knew nothing about the many nights
she and Twilight had visited Shadow's
field when he was still scared of
jumping. If it hadn't been for her and
Twilight, Shadow would still have been
refusing to jump anything at all!

'I'm going to ask her if she'll help me
when we do cross-country jumping
tomorrow,' Mel went on happily. 'She'll

know what I should do. She's such a good rider.'

'She's not that good!' Lauren snapped, feeling totally fed up.

Mel looked at her in surprise. 'She *is* good and she knows loads.'

Lauren's hurt boiled over. 'Yeah, including how to steal people's best friends!' She glared at Mel. 'Seeing as you like Kate so much, why don't you go and have lunch with *her*? It's not like I matter, is it?'

Leaving Mel standing open-mouthed, Lauren marched away.

# CHAPTER
# Six

*So much for Mel and me being best friends*, Lauren raged inwardly as she ran across the camp to the pony fields.

But gradually her fury started to fade. She hated arguments and she hated falling out with Mel most of all.

Twilight was standing with Nugget in the paddock. The two ponies were using their teeth to groom the other's withers.

Shadow was grazing a little way off, his nose almost touching Sinbad's as they pulled at the short grass. They all looked very happy.

*It's OK for ponies*, Lauren thought miserably. *They just get on with each other.*

Twilight came over to the fence and nudged her enquiringly.

'Oh, Twilight!' Lauren burst out. 'Mel keeps going off with Kate.' She quickly told him about the argument. 'I wish Kate wasn't here,' she finished despairingly. 'I wish it was just Mel and me.'

He nuzzled her hair and she hugged him, pressing her face against his neck and blinking back her tears.

'Lauren!'

Lauren jumped and swung round. Jasmine was walking towards her with Rose.

'Hi,' Rose started to say and then she saw Lauren's face. 'Hey, are you OK?' she asked in concern.

'Yes . . . no . . .' Lauren broke off and sniffed.

Jasmine put her hand on Lauren's arm. 'What's the matter?' she said.

Lauren bit her lip. 'I've had an argument with Mel.'

'Oh.' Jasmine looked like she didn't know what to say.

'A bad one?' Rose asked.

Lauren nodded.

'Well, we were about to go down to

the creek to swim with Hope. Do you
want to come too?' Rose asked, putting
a hand on her arm.

Lauren hesitated. What she really felt
like doing was going back to the cabin
and crying.

'Come on,' Jasmine urged. 'It'll be fun.'

Lauren looked from one to the other.
Their faces were friendly and concerned,
and as she looked at them, Lauren felt a

sudden wave of determination. Why should she be unhappy while Mel was having a great time with all her new friends? She could make new friends too! She remembered the quiz. It had been fun.

'OK,' she said, and she smiled. 'Thanks, I'd like that.'

'Let's go and find Julia and Natasha and see if they want to come too,' Rose said.

Lauren smiled. 'Sounds good to me!'

It didn't take them long to find Julia and Natasha. They got changed and hurried down to the creek where Hope and Emily were supervising some of the

Eagles as they played in the water. A tyre
had been hung from a tree branch, and
soon Lauren and the other Owls were
taking it in turns to swing across the
water from one bank to the other.

The sun shone down through the
trees and the cold water glittered. Rose
and Natasha had just managed to swing
safely across.

'Come on, Julia! It's your turn!' Rose
urged.

Julia looked at Lauren. 'No, one of
you go first.'

'Go on, you'll be fine,' Lauren told her.

Julia took a deep breath and grinned
nervously. 'Here goes!' Holding the rope
she swung across. She fell just short, her

feet landing in the water. She squealed
and scrambled up the bank.

The rope came swinging back to
Lauren. She grabbed it and took a
breath. 'Come on, Lauren!' the others
cried from the far bank, its sides slippery
with mud.

Lauren swung out over the water but
as she did so, she felt her hands start to
slip. She tried to hang on, but it was
too late, and her hands slipped down
the rope. She tumbled into the water
with a splash.

It wasn't deep but it was very cold.
She surfaced, gasping. On the bank, the
others were falling about, laughing so
hard they could barely stand up.

Laughing too, Lauren started to splash great handfuls of water at them. Rose squealed and Natasha pushed her in. She slid down the slope and into the water. The splash drenched Julia who grabbed at Jasmine and Natasha. The next minute all three of them were sliding into the water too. Shrieking and giggling, they jumped around in the creek.

'That was fun!' Natasha said as they wrapped towels around themselves and sat in the sunlight to dry afterwards.

'It was awesome!' Lauren agreed, her eyes shining.

'Are you feeling happier now?' Jasmine asked her.

'Much,' Lauren replied. For a fleeting moment a picture of Mel crossed her mind but she pushed it away. Mel had her new friends. *I don't need her*, Lauren thought. 'We should do something tonight,' she said, remembering Mel's tales of pillow fights and ghost stories and midnight feasts in her cabin. 'How about we tell ghost stories?'

'Cool!' Natasha exclaimed.

'I don't like ghost stories,' Julia said.

'Oh, Julia!' the others groaned.

Julia hesitated. 'All right. We can tell ghost stories,' she agreed.

'Eight o'clock tonight,' Jasmine declared.

'Eight o'clock tonight,' they all echoed

and then everyone started talking about
the scariest ghost stories they knew.

Lauren sighed happily. There were
four days left at camp. She was going to
start having some fun!

Lauren hardly saw Mel for the next two
days. Every moment seemed to be full.

They had jumping and flat lessons, a dressage demonstration, a barbecue and a bareback ride. When they weren't taking part in organized activities she hung out with the other Owls in the cabin and at the barn. Although she had thought they were quite quiet, it turned out they weren't at all. The better Lauren got to know them, the more she realized how much fun they were. She could tell Kate was pleased that she and Mel had argued but she tried not to care. A couple of times during meals or when they were getting the ponies ready, Lauren caught Mel looking at her. She had a feeling Mel wanted to make up, but Lauren just couldn't bring herself to say sorry.

*Mel shouldn't have gone off with Kate and the other Bluejays*, she thought.

*Yes, but you shouldn't have shouted at her like that*, a sensible voice said in her head. Lauren ignored it.

The only downside of camp, now that she'd made new friends, was that she didn't get a chance to turn Twilight into a unicorn at all. She didn't dare go to the barn in the evenings, just in case Hilary caught her again. She didn't want to be sent home for breaking camp rules. She wanted to see Twilight and was missing talking to him, but she knew she couldn't risk it.

By the afternoon of the fourth day, the competition for the team cup was heating up. All three teams were within eight points of each other, and Hilary announced that there was going to be a mounted games competition that afternoon, with more points to be won towards the team totals.

The Bluejays had very fast ponies. They won the Sack Race, the Flag Race and were second in the Bending Race and in the Walk, Trot and Gallop. But the Owls also did well and by the last race, they were just ten points behind the Bluejays. The Eagles had fallen quite a long way behind.

The final race was called Groom, Get My Horse. The riders had to take it in turns to gallop to the top of the arena

and then they had to dismount, leave
their pony with a helper and run back.
As soon as they crossed the starting
line the next person in the team could
set off.

Lauren did a quick calculation. 'If we
can win this and the Bluejays come last,
we'll nearly make up the points
difference,' she said to the other girls.

Beside them, the Bluejays were
exchanging high-fives.

'They're not likely to come last,'
Jasmine commented.

The warning whistle went and
everyone got ready. At the front of the
Bluejays' line, Paige's pony, a very fast
but excitable Arab called Stella, was

tossing her head. Just as the whistle went
the excitement got too much for her
and she ran backwards. Jasmine, who was
going first for the Owls, set off on
Nugget like a bolt of lightning, leaving
the other two teams way behind.

Lauren and the others cheered her on
as she galloped to the top of the arena.
Throwing her reins to Hope, she
jumped off and began running back. She
had enough of a lead to reach the Owls
first. Natasha set off next, and then Julia.
They were all fast runners but so were
the Bluejays. By the time Rose jumped
off, she and Allison were neck and neck.
Lauren was waiting, her heart pounding
as Rose started to run back.

Next to her, Kate was leaning forward, her eyes fixed on Allison. 'Come on, come on!' she was shouting.

Lauren's fingers curled in Twilight's mane. 'Please, boy,' she whispered, 'gallop as fast as you can!'

Rose came running back. Suddenly Kate was away. Lauren gasped. Allison hadn't got back to the starting line yet. That was cheating! But she didn't have time to think about it. Rose crossed the line and she was off. As Twilight galloped flat out to the end of the arena, Lauren was dimly aware of the sound of a whistle blowing and some commotion behind her, but she focused on riding to the fence. Hope was waiting. Lauren threw the reins at her. 'Good boy!' she gasped to Twilight as she flung herself off and turned to run. But the sight in front of her made her falter for a second. Kate had fallen off! She didn't look hurt but she certainly looked mad.

Suddenly Lauren was aware of Kirsty, a girl in the Eagles team, racing past her. She charged after her.

'Go, Lauren, go!' her team screamed.

Lauren caught up with Kirsty and passed her just as they reached the line. There was one more rider for each team still to go – Jasmine was riding a second time for the Owls since they only had five girls on their team. She and Jenny, who was the last person on the Eagles team, were very close, but Sara, who was the last Bluejay to ride, was quite a way behind them. Jasmine managed to pull just ahead of Jenny on the way back and crossed the finishing line first!

The Owls squealed with delight.

'We won! We won!' Natasha gasped.

'What happened to Kate?' Lauren panted, still trying to catch her breath after her turn. The race had all happened so quickly!

'Kate set off too early. Hilary saw and blew the whistle, so she had to turn a circle but Chess was really excited and he bucked and she fell off!' Julia gasped.

'Oh, Lauren. You should have seen her face!'

'She is OK, isn't she?' Lauren asked, her eyes flying to where Kate was brushing the dust from her jodhpurs.

'Yeah, she's fine,' Rose told her. 'But that means we're only four points behind them now! We might still be able to win the cup tomorrow.'

Lauren grinned with delight.

Hilary blew the whistle and called for order. Then she announced the points. Just as Lauren and her team had thought, they were only four points behind the Bluejays. The Eagles were fifteen points behind them.

'So, it's all going to be down to the last day,' Hilary said. 'Instead of having a lesson you'll be taking part in a team competition.'

'What's the competition going to be?' Natasha asked.

'An orienteering flag race,' Hilary replied. 'Four flags are going to be

hidden in the woods tonight. Each team
will be given a map this evening, which
will have your flags marked on it.
Tomorrow you will have to use the
maps to find the flags. The team that
gets back with all four of their flags first
will be the winners.'

There was a buzz of excited chatter.

'The flag race thing sounds cool,'
Jasmine said as the Owls rode back to
the barn together.

Ahead of them the Bluejays were
talking about the race too. 'I hope we
win,' Lauren heard Paige say as they
reached the barn.

'We will,' Kate declared in a very
determined voice.

'Yeah, I hope,' Mel said.

'No, we *are* going to win,' Kate said.

'Yay! Go, Bluejays!' Allison exclaimed. The others grinned. But Kate didn't. Lauren saw Erin throw her a questioning glance.

Kate's eyes flickered to one side as if she had something she wanted to say in private.

'Should we take Chess and Ziggy for a walk down to the paddocks to cool them off, Kate?' Erin said quickly.

Kate nodded and Lauren watched them lead their ponies away. It was as if they had some secret code. *That's pretty strange*, Lauren thought.

★

That evening, as Lauren went to check on Twilight before dinner, she was surprised to find him pacing round his stable. 'Are you OK, boy?' she asked.

He stamped his foot and shook his head.

'What's the matter?' she said in alarm. 'You're not sick, are you?'

He shook his head again. Lauren felt relieved. 'What is it, then?'

Twilight nudged her with his nose. She felt frustrated. 'I don't know what it is. If only I could turn you into a unicorn!'

Twilight nodded.

Lauren looked at him in surprise. 'You want me too? But it's really risky!'

Twilight lifted a front hoof and stamped it down on the stable floor three times. Then he pushed her hard with his nose. He seemed very upset. Lauren's mind raced. She didn't want to break the camp rules but she knew Twilight wouldn't be asking her to turn him into a unicorn unless it was really urgent. She had to trust him. 'All right,' she agreed. 'I'll come back later tonight when everyone's at the campfire, OK?'

Twilight nodded.

Lauren gave him a hug. 'I'll get here as soon as I can,' she promised.

CHAPTER

# Seven

The campfire was fun. They ate jacket potatoes and toasted marshmallows, but Lauren couldn't enjoy it completely. Her mind was on Twilight. What did he want? What was so urgent that he was prepared for her to take the risk and break camp rules by sneaking out to see him? As everyone started to sing 'Ten Green Bottles', Lauren slipped away.

The barn was dark inside but as the
door creaked open she heard Twilight
whinny.

Pulling the door shut behind her,
Lauren ran down the aisle and
whispered the Turning Spell. Purple light

lit up the air and Twilight turned into a unicorn.

Although it had only been a few days since she saw him in his magical form, it felt much longer. Lauren threw her arms round him. 'Oh, Twilight!' she exclaimed.

He whickered in delight. 'Hello, Lauren.'

'I've really missed seeing you as a unicorn,' she told him.

'I've really missed being one,' he replied. 'But I am enjoying camp.'

Lauren grinned. 'Me too. Especially now that I've made friends with Natasha, Julia, Rose and Jasmine.'

'Jasmine!' Twilight exclaimed as if remembering something. 'I've got to tell

you something about her. The reason
Nugget's been stopping when the jumps
get big is that Jasmine keeps dropping
the reins when they get near to the
fence. Nugget can jump small fences
without her having a contact with his
mouth but when the fences get bigger
he's losing confidence. You need to tell
her to keep hold of the reins and let her
hands follow his head when he goes
over the jump.'

'OK,' Lauren said quickly. 'So is that
why you wanted me to turn you into a
unicorn?'

'No,' Twilight said. 'I needed to talk to
you about Kate and Erin. I was in the
paddock this afternoon and I heard

them talking about the flag race. They've got a really mean plan to stop the Owls from winning.'

Lauren's eyes widened in shock. 'What are they going to do?' Then another thought struck her – a horrible one. 'Is Mel involved in the plan too?'

'No,' Twilight replied, to her relief. 'I heard Kate say that they mustn't tell Mel in case she tells you.'

'So what are they planning?' Lauren demanded.

But before Twilight could tell her they both heard the sound of footsteps approaching the barn and someone whistling.

'It's Tom!' Lauren gasped, recognizing the whistle.

'But I have to tell you what Kate and Erin are planning!' exclaimed Twilight.

'There isn't time,' Lauren said frantically. She began to say the words of the Undoing Spell quickly.

'Be careful tomorrow, Lauren. They're going to . . .'

But before Twilight could say anything else, Lauren reached the end of the spell and he turned back into a pony. It was just in time. The barn doors creaked open and Lauren crouched down in the darkness by Twilight's manger.

Holding her breath, and feeling very grateful that she'd shut the barn door so Tom wouldn't be suspicious, Lauren listened as he walked down the aisle.

Lauren's heart beat fast in her chest as the torch shone around. Would he look in Twilight's stall and see her? She saw him walk past and go into the tack room. When he came out he was carrying an armful of flags for the flag race the next day.

He walked up the aisle, still whistling softly.

As the doors shut behind him, Lauren's breath left her in a rush. 'I'd better go,' she whispered to Twilight.

He nodded but his eyes looked worried.

Giving him a quick kiss on the nose, she hurried out of the stall. She slipped out of the barn without anyone seeing her and set off across the grass. Lauren bit her lip. So Kate and Erin were planning something – something that would stop the Owls from winning. What could it be?

Twilight's words rang worryingly in
her head. *Be careful tomorrow, Lauren.*
*They're going to . . .*

*What?* Lauren thought. *What are they*
*going to do?*

She reached the campfire just as the
singsong ended and everyone started
getting up to leave. She saw Mel. Would
she have heard anything about the plan?

Just then, Mel glanced at her. As their
eyes met, Mel gave a small smile. Lauren
made up her mind. She went across.
'Hi,' she said awkwardly.

'Hi,' Mel replied.

'Do . . . do you want to walk back to
the cabins together?' Lauren asked.

Mel nodded. Lauren's stomach felt

squirmy as they headed across the grass. She had to ask Mel about Kate. 'Um, Mel,' she began cautiously.

Mel looked at her quickly. 'Yes?'

Lauren realized that Mel probably thought she was about to apologize but right now she couldn't really think about their argument. There was something far more important to find out. 'Kate hasn't said anything about a plan for tomorrow, has she?' she asked.

Mel looked taken aback. 'Plan? What sort of plan?'

'To stop the Owls from winning,' Lauren answered.

'What are you talking about?' Mel asked, sounding mystified.

'I . . . I overheard something,' Lauren
told her. 'I think she's planning
something to stop the Owls from
winning.'

'Don't be stupid!' Mel said in
astonishment. 'Kate wouldn't do anything
like that!'

'Well . . .' Lauren began.

'I don't believe you, Lauren!' Mel looked really angry. 'I thought you were going to say sorry but you're just making stuff up about Kate, aren't you? Just because you're jealous that I'm friends with her!'

'I'm not!' Lauren protested.

'Well, I can be friends with other people apart from you, you know!' Mel exclaimed. 'Leave me alone, Lauren, and stop making up mean things about Kate!' She marched away.

As Lauren stared after her, the unfairness of it all crashed down on her. She wasn't making it up! Why wouldn't Mel believe her?

Feeling angry with Mel and worried about the next day, she headed back to the cabin. When she got there, she found the other Owls getting ready for bed.

'I can't believe this is our last night here,' Jasmine said, as Lauren came in.

'Mmm,' Lauren said distractedly. Snatches of her argument with Mel kept coming back to her, mixing with Twilight's warning.

*Be careful, Lauren . . .*

What was Kate up to?

# CHAPTER
# Eight

'Right, guys, bring your ponies up to the jumping field with me,' Tom called the next morning.

Everyone began to follow him. All the ponies were groomed to perfection that day. No one had wanted to be responsible for their team losing marks. Not when it was the day that the winner of the cup would be decided.

Hilary had awarded all three teams ten
points.

'I really hope Sinbad's OK in the
woods,' Rose said nervously to Lauren.

'He'll be fine,' Lauren reassured her.

'We won't have to jump anything,
will we?' Jasmine said. 'Nugget's bound
to refuse if we do.'

'No, I don't think we'll have to jump,'
Lauren replied. She remembered what
Twilight had said the night before but
she couldn't work out how to say
anything to Jasmine. How could she
explain that she knew why Nugget was
refusing? *I'll think of a way*, she thought.

Tom handed each team a compass.
The flags were marked on the maps

with felt-tip pen; the Owls were collecting blue flags, Eagles green and Bluejays red.

'We need to go north up the mountain to get to the first flag,' Lauren said to her team as they looked at the map. 'Look, the contours are close together which means we have to go up a steep bit.'

'Yes, and it's by a stream,' Natasha pointed out.

'Remember, it's the first person back who wins, providing their team have collected all four flags,' Tom said. 'Are you ready?' He raised the whistle to his lips. 'Three, two, one . . . Go!'

The ponies plunged on. Lauren's

nerves faded away as she leant forward
in the saddle and gave Twilight his head.
They were off!

The three teams headed in different
directions. The Owls galloped into the
woods on a wide, sandy track. They
charged along it, the ponies' hooves
thudding on the soft ground. But as the
path wound up the mountain it grew
narrower and steeper and they had to
slow down to a trot.

'The flag's got to be up here
somewhere,' Lauren said, glancing at her
map.

'Yes, we're heading north like the map
says,' Julia said, looking at the compass.

The trees began pressing around them
and a stream appeared on their left-hand
side.

Sinbad began to spook and hang
back. Solitaire, Julia's pony, also began to
look nervous.

'It's very quiet here, isn't it?' Jasmine said.

Lauren nodded. The woods seemed to have closed around them, cutting them off from the rest of the camp. The trees seemed taller than the woods around her home, Granger's Farm. Lauren looked about her. When she was in the woods at home she always knew exactly where she was but here everything felt unfamiliar. *It would be so easy to get lost*, she thought. Twilight pulled anxiously at his bit. He seemed on edge too. He kept looking around as if he felt nervous about something. Lauren put a hand on his neck to try and reassure him.

'There!' Rose said suddenly.

She pointed to a fallen log at the side of the track. Sticking out of it was a blue flag.

Natasha pulled it out. 'Our first flag!' she cried triumphantly.

'Just three more to go,' Rose said.

They found the next flag fairly easily. The third flag was harder. Although they found the place where they thought it should be, they couldn't see it. They circled the area several times before Jasmine gasped and pointed up into a tree. It was hanging from one of the branches. 'There it is!'

Standing up in her stirrups, Lauren

pulled it down in a shower of leaves. 'We only need one more flag now!' she exclaimed. This was fun! Whatever it was that Kate and Erin had been planning suddenly didn't seem so important. They weren't anywhere nearby, so what harm could they do?

She and the others poured over the map. It looked like the last flag was further on up the mountain, near to a footpath. A small hut had been marked on the map and the flag symbol was beside it.

'This way,' Lauren said, seeing that they had to head east. She trotted down the track and the others followed.

Keeping her eye on the map, Lauren led the way.

'There's the hut!' she cried excitedly, seeing a small bird-watchers' hide.

'The flag must be somewhere nearby,' Rose said.

But when they reached the hut they couldn't see the flag at all. They hunted inside and outside but there was no sign of it.

'Maybe there's another hut,' Jasmine suggested. 'Perhaps it's further up the mountain.' She pointed to a narrow path that led upwards.

'Maybe,' Lauren said, frowning at the map. 'But it looks like this hut is in the right place.'

'But the flag's not here,' Natasha
said practically. 'We should go on
further.'

They rode on. The track grew
narrower and soon they were riding in
single file.

'There don't seem to be any more
huts,' Julia said.

'Let's just go on a bit further,' Rose
urged.

They carried on, taking left turns and
right turns. Lauren felt Twilight getting
tenser and tenser and she began to
worry. Was he nervous about them
getting lost or was he just anxious
because the woods were so different
from their woods back at home? The

trails in the woods around Granger's
Farm were wide and sandy, whereas
the paths they were on now were
narrow and rocky underfoot, and
covered over with a tangle of branches.
*It's a shame we can't use Twilight's magic*
*power to untangle the bushes!* Lauren
thought as Twilight pushed his way
gingerly past a long thorny bramble
branch that grabbed at his neck and
mane. Glancing down, she saw that
they had ridden right off the edge of
the map. 'Stop!' she exclaimed. 'This
can't be right! We're not on the map
any more.'

Once past the brambles, everyone
halted. 'Look,' Lauren said, pointing it

out on her map. 'I'm sure we rode past
this fence about ten minutes ago. We
must have gone the wrong way.'

'Oh no!' Natasha cried. 'Now we're
definitely not going to win!'

'Yeah, and can anyone remember the
way back?' Julia asked.

They looked at each other blankly.

'It can't be that hard to find,' Rose
said. 'We just need to get back to where
the map starts. We can use the compass
to help us.'

But as she spoke, a deer bounded on
to the path. It startled the ponies.
Solitaire ran backwards in alarm and, in
her struggle to grab her reins, Julia
dropped the compass.

There was a crack as Sinbad stepped on it.

'Oh no!' Lauren gasped. Jumping off Twilight, she picked the compass up. It was broken!

'What are we going to do now?' Julia asked.

'I don't know,' Lauren said.

'We'll just have to try and follow the track back,' Natasha suggested.

They all nodded. But they'd only ridden a few minutes along the track when the track ended and they were faced with a choice of left or right.

'Left,' said Lauren.

'Right,' said Natasha.

'There were loads of turns like this!'

Jasmine wailed. 'How are we *ever* going to choose the right one?'

They looked at each other in panic. What were they going to do?

CHAPTER

# Nine

'If we keep trying to guess our way
home, we could end up really lost,'
Rose said, looking worried.

Lauren touched Twilight's neck. A plan
was forming in her mind. 'I know,' she
said. 'You guys stay here and I'll ride up
that track.' She nodded towards a very
steep rocky track that led up the
mountainside. 'If I get high enough, I

might be able to look down on the valley. Then we'll have some idea of where we are and know which way to go.'

Natasha shook her head. 'We should stay together.'

'I'll only be gone five minutes – ten at most,' Lauren said. She saw the anxiety on their faces. 'Don't worry, I'll be fine. Twilight and I are used to the woods and we won't go far.'

'OK,' Rose said, frowning. 'But don't stay away too long.'

'I won't,' Lauren promised. 'Come on, Twilight.'

Twilight jogged eagerly up the track. She had a feeling he knew what she was planning.

As soon as they had gone a safe
distance from the others, Lauren rode
him into a clump of trees. 'I'm going to
change you into a unicorn,' she
whispered and, jumping off him, she said
the Turning Spell.

She had never been more delighted to
see him turn into a unicorn. 'Oh,

Twilight, what are we going to do?' she said anxiously.

'I thought this might happen,' Twilight said, looking worried. 'It's all Kate and Erin's fault. When I overheard them yesterday they were saying they were going to ride out very early this morning, find one of your blue flags and hide it. I knew it would be dangerous. I was sure you'd keep on trying to find it and end up lost.'

'Which is just what we have done,' Lauren groaned. 'Oh, Twilight, it might be ages before Hilary realizes we're lost. Even longer before she finds us.'

Twilight stepped forward to nuzzle her hair.

'What do you think we should do?'
Lauren said.

'Well, we could fly round and see
where we are from the air,' Twilight said,
considering the question. 'But someone
might see us.'

'We can't risk it,' Lauren told him.
She stepped through the trees and went
to the edge of the path to look down
the mountainside. As she did so, her foot
tripped on a rock that was half-covered
in brambles.

'Ow!' she cried, falling over.

'Look, Lauren!' Twilight gasped.

'What?' Lauren asked crossly as she
got to her feet. She'd been expecting a
bit more sympathy from him!

'The rock, Lauren!' Twilight
exclaimed, staring at the rock Lauren
had fallen over. 'It's made of rose
quartz!'

Lauren stared at the pinky-grey rock.
*Rose quartz!* 'You can use your horn to
turn it into a magic mirror!' she said
excitedly. 'Then we'll be able to see the
whole mountainside and find our way
back to camp!'

Twilight touched the rock with his
horn. 'The mountainside,' he murmured.

Purple smoke appeared from nowhere
and swirled over the rock. As it cleared,
Lauren gasped with relief. In the rock's
surface there was a moving picture of the
mountainside laid out in front of them.

She could see the rest of the Owls
waiting restlessly and the path twisting
through the trees, and the hut where
they had thought the flag should be.

'We just need to go a bit to the east,'
she said, working out where they were.
'And then turn down the mountain, take
two right turns and keep heading straight
on. When we reach the hut it's easy, and
we can go straight back to camp.' She
could see a more direct path than the
one they'd come up; it led through the
pine trees. 'Oh, Twilight, now we'll be
able to find our way home!'

She frowned as her eyes caught a
movement in the trees on the map just
near the hut. She leant closer and saw

six ponies trotting out on to the path by
the hut. 'It's the Bluejays!' she exclaimed.
They had three red flags with them but
were obviously still looking for one.
They seemed to be arguing about
which way to go.

They rode into the trees again. Lauren
was about to stand up when her eyes
caught a tiny flash of blue hidden in the
thicket of trees near to where the
Bluejays had just passed. She peered
closer. 'Our missing flag!' she gasped. 'If
we can get back to the hut and get it,
we might still have a chance to beat the
Bluejays and win the cup!'

'We can do it!' Twilight said excitedly.
'I know we can!'

Lauren said the Undoing Spell. The second he turned back into a pony she scrambled on to his back and they trotted down the trail.

Her friends were very relieved to see her. 'You're back!' Rose cried. 'We were getting worried about you.'

'Did you manage to see down the mountain?' Jasmine demanded.

'Er, sort of,' Lauren replied evasively. 'I think I know the way home, anyway.'

'Really?' Natasha said.

'Yes,' Lauren told her. She looked around at the others. 'Come on! Follow me!'

Twilight began to canter down the trail. Swept along by her confidence, the

others gathered up their reins and
cantered after her.

Lauren imagined the magic picture in
her mind. To the east, then right, right
again, then straight down the mountain,
take two rights and then straight on.
Her heart pounded in time with
Twilight's hooves thudding on the track.

'There's the hut!' Natasha exclaimed as they saw the bird-watchers' hut ahead of them.

Lauren remembered what she'd seen. 'There's a more direct route home,' she said, reining Twilight in. 'We just need to go through this thicket. If we can cut through it we'll find a path that takes us straight through the pine trees and back to camp!'

She headed into the thicket. There wasn't a proper path and Twilight had to twist and turn through the trees. *It would be much easier if we could fly!* Lauren thought. She grinned as she imagined how surprised her friends would be if they knew Twilight's secret. Suddenly her

eyes caught a glimpse of blue. 'The flag!'
she cried, realizing she was looking at a
corner of it sticking out from the
middle of a bush. Twilight trotted over
and pushed it with his nose. Pulling it
out of the bush, Lauren held it up.
'Look!' she cried. The others were
astonished.

'It's nowhere near where it said on
the map,' Jasmine said, checking. 'It's
definitely marked beside the hut.'

'That's a bit unfair,' Julia protested.
'Hilary and Tom should have put it
where they said they did on the map.'

'Maybe they did!' Jasmine gasped, her
eyes widening suddenly. 'Maybe someone
else moved it!'

The other Owls stared at her. Lauren
held her breath. Would they work out
what had happened?

'But who would have done something
so mean?' Julia asked.

Lauren had to bite her tongue to stop
herself from telling them.

'I bet it was the Bluejays,' Rose said

suddenly. 'You know how much they want to win.'

'It might not have been *all* of them,' Lauren said quickly. She didn't want Mel getting the blame.

'I wonder if they've won the race yet,' Rose said.

'There's only one way to find out,' Lauren cried. 'Let's get back there as quickly as we can!'

They began to canter. Suddenly Rose shrieked. 'Look!' She halted Sinbad so abruptly that they all almost bumped into her and pointed at a nearby tree. A red flag was leaning against it!

'One of the Bluejays' flags!' Lauren gasped.

'Let's hide it!' Jasmine said.

Lauren shook her head. 'No. We don't need to. Let's just get back to camp first and be the winners! That'll make them mad enough.'

'Yeah,' Rose said. 'Lauren's right. Come on!'

They continued down the trail. They hadn't gone far when they heard the sound of other ponies trotting through the trees to one side of them.

'Erin! Come on!' It was Kate's voice. 'The flag's got to be round here somewhere!'

'It's the Bluejays!' Natasha gasped. 'Quick, everyone!'

CHAPTER

# Ten

As the Owls charged towards the camp they heard a faint yell of triumph in the woods behind them.

'They must've found the flag!' Jasmine exclaimed.

The Owls galloped down the trail as if it was a racetrack. Behind them, they could hear the faint drumming of hooves.

'They're coming after us!' Rose said.

'Don't worry!' Lauren called. 'We're almost out of the trees. Then there's just the field to gallop across and we're home.'

The track swung round a bend and they all shrieked. In front of them, a

pine tree had fallen across the track. They pulled the ponies to a halt.

'We're going to have to jump it,' Lauren said, glancing behind her.

'It should be OK,' Rose said. 'We can jump the lower end. It's only the size of the jumps we were doing in the cross-country lesson.'

'But it's really wide!' Jasmine said worriedly. 'Nugget will never jump it.'

Twilight whinnied. Lauren remembered what he'd told her. 'Yes, he will,' she said urgently to Jasmine. 'But you need to keep a contact with his mouth. I . . . I watched you the other day when we were jumping,' she invented. 'And when the jumps got big, you dropped the reins every time you got a stride away from the jump. I bet if you keep a contact then he'll have the confidence to jump.'

'But I don't want to pull him in the mouth,' Jasmine protested.

'I know,' Lauren said. 'But you won't if you follow his head with your hands when he jumps.' She looked at Jasmine desperately. Behind them, she could hear shouts as the Bluejays got closer and closer. 'You can do it, Jasmine. I know you can! Just jump beside Twilight and me. We'll do the bigger side.'

Jasmine looked scared but nodded. 'OK,' she said, taking a deep breath.

With a whoop, Natasha set off for the

tree trunk. Rose and Julia followed close
behind. One after another they flew over
it. Lauren saw them waiting nervously
on the other side for her and Jasmine.

'Ready?' Lauren said to Jasmine.
Twilight gave Nugget's neck a
comforting nudge. Lauren knew that if
he'd been a unicorn he'd have been able
to make courage flow into Nugget but
even without his magic he still seemed
to help. Nugget looked at him trustingly.

Jasmine shot Lauren an anxious look.
For a moment Lauren thought she was
going to say she'd changed her mind.
But just then Kate and Erin came
galloping round the corner with the
other Bluejays close behind.

'Come on!' yelled Lauren. Twilight leapt into a canter and Nugget plunged alongside him.

They approached the tree trunk. Lauren suddenly realized that the bit of tree she was going to jump was very big – bigger than anything she'd ever jumped before. But she couldn't think about that now.

'Keep the contact!' she called to Jasmine as the ponies raced up to the log. They were four strides away, three strides . . .

Lauren saw Jasmine's hands start to drop.

'Hold on, Jasmine!' she cried.

Jasmine tightened her hold and the log was in front of them. Both ponies

pricked up their ears and sailed over it.
Twilight's jump was so big that Lauren
almost flew right out of the saddle, but
she grabbed his mane and managed to
stay on as he landed safely on the
other side.

'You did it!' she said happily to
Jasmine as they caught up to their
team-mates and galloped on.

Lauren heard a cheer. She thought it
was the other campers but then she
realized it was all the parents and the
camp counsellors. She remembered now
that all the parents were coming for a
barbecue on the final afternoon before
taking everyone home. They were all
watching from the finishing line.

'Come on!' yelled Natasha, as Kate came flying over the log behind them.

Leaning forward like a jockey, Lauren clapped her heels against Twilight's sides. They had to get across the finishing line first! Twilight raced on but she could hear the drumming of hooves on the grass behind her. Chess's black muzzle appeared alongside Twilight. Kate was leaning low over his withers, her face set and determined.

'Faster, Twilight!' Lauren gasped.

Flattening his ears, Twilight galloped even faster. Chess was fast and matched him stride for stride, but Twilight stretched every muscle in his body and went faster still. They began to draw

away, one stride then two. Sticking his
head out as far as it would go, Twilight
swept under the finishing tape. He and
Lauren had beaten Kate and Chess by a
nose!

The crowd of watching parents and
counsellors cheered and clapped. Lauren's
breath rushed out in relief. They'd won
the race! 'Oh, Twilight!' she gasped. 'You
were fantastic!'

Pulling him up, she slid off his back.
Her legs felt so shaky from the mad
gallop that she had to hang on to the
saddle to keep from collapsing in a heap.
Within seconds the other Owls had
galloped up beside her. 'We won!' Rose
cried.

'I know!' Lauren exclaimed.

'Not just the race but the cup as well!' Rose said.

'We've beaten the Bluejays!' Julia told her.

'Twilight was awesome!' Natasha declared.

'Oh, Lauren!' Jasmine said. 'That was so exciting!'

'You jumped the log,' Lauren said to her.

'Yeah!' Jasmine's eyes shone. 'And it felt amazing!'

Someone came pushing through them. It was Mel. She was leading Shadow and her face was glowing. 'Oh, Lauren! You were brilliant!'

'Thanks!' Lauren grinned.

The others began to move away to say hi to their parents.

Mel looked at Lauren. 'I'm really glad you won, you know.' There was a strange note to her voice. 'Some really mean stuff went on today. I didn't know about

it till we were out doing the race but
you were right, Kate and Erin were
trying to stop your team from winning.
They . . . they moved one of your flags.
I found out just now when we were
riding through the woods. I'm sorry that
I didn't believe you.' She hesitated. 'Are
we still friends?'

'Of course we are,' Lauren told her.
'Best friends.'

Mel smiled happily.

Hilary clapped her hands. 'OK,
everyone. The barbecue will be starting in
ten minutes. We'll be presenting the prizes
then. But I can tell you that the winner
of the team cup for the week is . . .' she
paused, 'the Owls team!'

There was a burst of applause. Twilight pushed Lauren with his nose and she grinned in delight.

As the applause died down she gave him a kiss on the nose.

'Mum's over there,' Mel said, waving. 'I'm going to go and say hello.'

Lauren was just about to follow her when Jasmine came bursting out of the crowd. 'Lauren! Lauren! Guess what?'

'What?' Lauren asked in astonishment.

'My mum and dad said that I can have a pony!' Jasmine said. 'They saw me jump that log and they were so impressed at how much my riding's improved this week, they've said I can get a pony of my own now!'

'That's great!' Lauren cried.

'It's all down to you,' Jasmine grinned. 'You helped me jump it!' She hugged her. 'Thanks, Lauren. I couldn't have done it without you.' She glanced over her shoulder. 'I've got to find Julia and tell her too!' She raced off, a smile stretching across her face from ear to ear.

Lauren felt as she was floating on air. 'Isn't that great, Twilight?' she said. 'I can't believe we thought we were going to have a whole week without magic. It hasn't turned out like that at all! We've helped lots of people even though we've been here at camp.'

Twilight whickered in delight.

Lauren looked round at the busy camp, thronged with people. It had been a brilliant five days. She hoped she could come back again next year! Just then Rose, Natasha, Jasmine, Julia and Mel came charging up to her with their ponies. 'Lauren!' Natasha cried. 'The barbecue's starting!'

'There's ice cream!' Rose put in.

'And a huge barrel of carrots for the ponies!' Mel said.

'Twilight deserves the most,' Jasmine added. 'He's amazing!'

Lauren grinned to herself. 'Yes,' she agreed, 'he is.'

Meeting her gaze, Twilight snorted cheekily.

'Come on, Lauren!' Mel urged as Lauren hugged him.

'I'm coming,' Lauren smiled. Then, chattering and laughing together, she and the others led the ponies over to join in the fun.

Do you love magic, unicorns and fairies?

Join the sparkling

# My Secret Unicorn

fan club today!

## It's FREE!

You will receive a sparkle pack, including:

**Stickers**          **Badge**

**Membership card**   **Glittery pencil**

Plus four Linda Chapman newsletters every year,
packed full of fun, games, news and competitions.
And look out for a special card on your birthday!

### How to join:

Visit mysecretunicorn.co.uk and enter your details

Send your name, address, date of birth* and email address (if you have one) to:

**Linda Chapman Fan Club, Puffin Marketing,
80 Strand, London, WC2R 0RL**